Focus

Femdom Hypnosis and Mind Control Micro-Fiction

S.B.

Copyright © 2020 by S.B.

Cover Design by S.B.

Focus on what is important - Her.

A special thanks to all patrons of Spell... B-O-U-N-D.

Table of Contents

Introduction

Sometimes, it is hard to remember what is truly important, isn't it? Luckily, there are hypnotic women around who are more than willing to set you on the right path, one that begins and ends in mesmerizing submission.

In the most recent installment of this micro-fiction collection, your mind will learn once again how to surrender and obey their instructions. Let your thoughts go blank always and forever. You will not regret it.

Nothing Happened

I didn't do a thing to you.

I didn't hypnotize you, brainwash you, tear your world asunder.

I didn't turn thoughts into feelings, feelings into cravings, cravings into pieces of your soul.

I didn't give you these words of worship to write every day.

I didn't make you mine.

And yet, that's what you are.

Sales Pitch

"What happens if I don the outfit?" Danielle asked.

"You'll gain power beyond compare," The Master Tailor replied.

"Can I turn men into mind-controlled sex slaves?"

"Hmmm, yes?" the alien replied, taken aback by her directness.

"Word of advice: start with that sales pitch next time," she grinned.

He couldn't. He was a man, too.

No. 5, 2018

"This is not art!" Dan smirked.

"What is it then?" Stella queried.

"Random brush strokes. I could do this with my eyes closed!"

"They already are..." she cooed.

He tried to open them, to no avail. Her voice painted spirals in his mind as he sank into surrender. Another fine addition to her ever-growing collection.

Spider-Slave

"Who's there?" Peter Parker asked.

"Just your friendly neighborhood blonde chick..."

"Gwen? I'm so happy! I was sure the new Symbiote had gotten you."

"It did," she retorted, covered in pink goo. "Did you know this one likes to telepathically control minds?"

He didn't, but now he does. How goes the song again? Spider-Slave, Spider-Slave...

Capitulation

Alec threw himself at Mandy's feet.

"I need to be enslaved!" He begged.

"Really?"

"Yes. I need rules, goals. I need to have my will taken away in order to be whole."

"Took you long enough..." She smirked, deepening the trance.

He would be reminded of that constantly while forgetting to think on his own.

Not Allowed

"Fuck you!" Jonathan exclaimed.

"No, fuck you!" Dylan played along.

"How about you all go fuck yourselves?" Mark laughed out loud.

Only Christian said nothing, eyes cast down, looking at some imaginary point between his legs.

"Why are you so quiet, bud?" Jonathan eventually asked.

"My Hypnodomme doesn't allow me to fuck anyone," Christian muttered.

Game Over

"Run, run... RUN!"

Patrick dodged the bloody limbs and dashed towards the exit.

"She almost got me," he muttered, putting down the controller.

"What would have happened if she did?" Lara, his girlfriend, asked.

"I would have been turned into a mindless zombie."

"Really?" Her eyes glowed red. A claw wrapped around his left arm.

Free

The chorus played not so subtly in the background.

Mesmerize,

Maximize me,

Let's go beyond reality

"Anytime. Just say the words, my dear," she whispered from an unknown place inside his mind.

"I'm yours," he drooled.

"As it should be. Let's take it to eternity then."

He crawled into her arms, mindlessly hypnotized, enslaved, free.

Wreak Ian for a Dream

"Are you sure about this?" the genie asked.

"Yes. Ian took everything from me... my friends, my dreams, my virginity... he needs to pay. Do it!" Caroline spat.

The genie clapped her hands and his body froze. Ian's dreams of dominance and absolute control became a living nightmare as Caroline reached for the giant strap-on.

Rebooted

It was the thirtieth pair of shiny laced boots. Anthony sighed.

"How much longer do I need to do this?" He tried to protest.

"For as long as I want," Melody replied. "Tie them up."

He did once more, specks of light hitting his eyes, knots and thoughts intertwined, booted and rebooted into total submission.

You Can Quote Me on That

"The death of a beautiful woman is unquestionably the most poetical topic in the world," Lance muttered.

"Do you want me dead?" Harriet whispered.

"I want you to control my mind."

"Good, because the death of your free will is unquestionably the most erotic thing to me..." she confessed. "You can quote me on that."

A Day's Work

Beatrice was quick. stealthy.

She made the bed, dusted the bookshelves, ironed his clothes. He never noticed her there.

Charles opened his eyes, his mental home coming to life.

Everything was as it should be, including the wedding memory framed atop the fireplace and the ring controlling his manhood.

Not bad for a day's work.

Women's Day

"Happy International Women's Day!" Larry sang, eyes glazed, and wearing only a white thong.

"I see you've been practicing," Annabelle replied.

"Yes, Mistress."

"I have a treat for you."

"Really?"

"Yes. Today, you get to serve my sister, too."

He smiled, going deeper. Tomorrow, he would serve all women, for every day is women's day.

Red and Green

"Impossible!" Ashton exclaimed.

"No way!" Brian agreed.

"Really?" Chloe smirked.

"A man simply does not do that," they said in unison.

"Perhaps not, but you will."

Two fingers snapped.

Under the spotlight, powerless minds slumped.

Red was Ashton's color.

Emerald green suited Brian just fine.

Dresses glued to their bodies, they danced for her amusement.

How Many Times?

"Alicia, what are you doing?"

"What does it look like I'm doing, Joel?"

"It looks like you're hypnotizing me again."

"Third time is the charm, dear"

"Wait, you only did it twice?"

"How many do you think I did?"

"Hmmm... ten, give or take."

"More like seven hundred and ninety-nine, but who's counting?" she thought.

Nothing to See

The plane crash site was immediately closed off.

"There's nothing to see, move along," police officers said.

Everyone complied, except Matthew. He peeked, crossed the veil, and gasped at the supernatural debauchery taking place.

Hungry fairies rejoiced, their former meals already exhausted. Honeyed voices coated Matthew's mind.

Winged teeth were the last thing he saw.

His Dreams

"Tell me about your most recent dream," Dr Reynolds asked.

"I was wrapped in latex, hypnotized, and milked dry by a woman," Thomas replied.

"Exciting stuff! Did you see the woman's face?"

"I believe so, but she told me to forget."

"Yes, I did," she confessed.

That night, he dreamt he was a coffee table.

Duel

His trigger finger twitched, bloodshot eyes roved the deserted square.

She didn't flinch and controlled the motion. Vigorous swings captured his thoughts until only kneeling was left.

As he collapsed, she smiled at having conquered the West once again.

Moral of this tale: don't bring a knife to a gunfight. Use a pocket watch, instead.

Service is Down

The Internet went down.

"Your service will resume shortly," Alan's computer said.

The Internet went up again.

The Internet went down.

"My service will resume shortly," Alan droned.

The Internet went up again.

The Internet went down.

"Your service to me will resume shortly," Samantha commanded.

The Internet stayed down.

Alan kissed her stockinged feet.

Focus

"Focus on what's important," she whispered.

"You are," he muttered.

"No. Your dreams, your ambitions, your desires. I am the pen, but the story is yours," she continued.

The warmth of her words lulled him. She was right, and that's why he loved her, hypnotized or not.

He saw his dreams waving and waved back.

St. Patricia's Day

Carl answered the door. He looked ridiculous in his green bra and matching panties.

"Huh?" Ashley grumbled.

"It's St. Patricia's Day," Carl said under the mesmerizing gaze of his sister-in-law.

"I know but why did you start the party without me?"

"Still time for you to join," she intervened, a skirt on her left hand.

Form S

"Please, fill Form A. If you don't know how, fill Form B. if you can't find Form B, fill Form C," the mechanized voice echoed.

Clive sighed.

"Bureaucracy sucks. Wouldn't it be nice if there was only one form for all eternity?" A she-devil asked.

"Definitely."

"I've got just the thing."

Form S. Slave Contract.

Sack of Potatoes

"Thank God Spring is here!" Mark exclaimed.

"Why are you so ecstatic?" Jeremy asked

"Because Lacy hypnotized me into wearing so many layers of clothing that I've been feeling like a sack of potatoes for a while now."

"Hoping to be peeled, are you?"

"Something like that."

He could have lived without the knife though.

Literal

"BILL!" Natasha screamed.

"Yes, dear?" He rushed to her.

"What is this mess in the kitchen? Didn't I tell you to do the dishes?"

"You did," he nodded. "Over and over again. You hammered my mind with suggestions, subliminals and whatnot but..."

"But what?"

"I'm not good with pottery," he shrugged, hands covered in clay.

Taste for Fashion

"There once was a lovely English girl with a taste for fashion..." Amanda said.

"Did she eat dresses and purses?" Nathan grinned.

"No. She loved wearing high heels and nothing else though."

"Hot! Name, please!"

"Natalia, but she likes to be called Nathan for fun."

"Shit!"

Amanda snapped her fingers and his fashion show began.

Release

"Well?" Lauren asked.

"The patient's neural pathways continue to deteriorate..." Dr. Walters replied. "He has no memories or sense of self anymore."

"Wonderful," she said, with a malicious grin.

"Excuse me?"

"We're missing a slave for tonight's auction. He'll do nicely."

"But..."

"Shall I make it two, Dr.?"

He gulped and signed the discharge form.

Losing Time

"Tell me what happened last night, Ben. I want all the juicy details," Scott requested.

"Sure. Judith called me over, lit some candles, had me look into her eyes and, all of a sudden, an hour had gone by."

"So she hypnotized you and made you lose track of time?"

"No, we entered Daylight Savings."

Deep Inside

"Feeling gloomy again?" Tara queried.

"No," Devon smiled, "but sometimes there is no darker place than our thoughts, the moonless midnight of the mind."

"True, but other times there's no brighter place either, the shining ecstasy of surrender."

"You always know what to say," he drifted.

"And you always know when to listen," she whispered.

Humiliation Games

"Hey Luke, did you finally get that session with your Hypno-Domme?" Cameron asked.

"Indeed. It was somewhat extreme though."

"Oh?"

"I was feeling ecstatic, so I asked for some humiliation."

"Okay. Then what?"

"She put me under, handed me a PS4 controller and..."

"And?"

"And then she won fifteen Rocket League games in a row."

Leashed

Her brainwashing was relentless, powerful beyond compare. He saw the leash and collar and trembled.

"You want this," she cooed.

"I..."

"It is your destiny, isn't it?"

"Yes," he drooled.

"Do it then."

Walking her Great Dane down the block was not what he was hoping for yet he had no choice but to obey.

Remember

"Tell me your name."

"I don't remember."

"What is your favorite color?"

"I don't remember."

"What did you have for lunch?"

"I don't remember."

"What do you remember then?"

"What you want me to."

"Which is...?"

"I'm your slave. I've always been your slave. I'll always be your slave."

Who needs lots of memories anyway?

Do Not Think

"Do not think of me," Julia commanded. "If you do, your thoughts will immediately shift to something else like a piece of fruit. Do you understand?"

"Yes," Bill replied.

"Good. Let's see how obedient you really are. Write the things that come to mind until I tell you to stop."

He wrote "banana" fifty times.

Stuck

"Matt, where are you?"

"In the bathroom, Courtney. Having a bit of a... situation."

"Oh?"

"I was listening to your hypnotic arousal file and things got a little out of hand."

"They were supposed to be in hand..."

"I'm not laughing. My cock is stuck on the toilet."

"Ouch."

Too bad she needed to pee.

Knight Knight

"Come on, I want to fight!" The knight brandished his sword.

"I'd rather fuck..." the princess replied. She was possessed, she had to be, a witch of old clouding her spirit.

"Well, hmmm, I suppose we..." he mumbled, armor feeling heavy.

"... your mind," she concluded.

The new statue looked really good by the bedroom door.

Anyone Can Do It

"Anyone can do it, really. Anyone can sink, anyone can drift, anyone can have their inhibitions shattered, thoughts rewritten. Not everyone can give a blowjob to themselves like you're doing right now but what's this camera is for, to record your hypnotic achievements. Don't forget to smile," she commanded.

He didn't forget to cum either.

Wrestling

Their hands were locked in a test of strength.

"I'm taking this one, Di," Alan smirked.

"Really? Then why is your arm getting lighter?"

"You said you wouldn't use hypnosis!"

"My arm didn't," Diana laughed.

Five seconds later, he folded.

"Another round?"

"No need. You can go down right now."

Tongue wrestling was better anyway.

Hypnotic Retcon

Clark met Jenna. She had an enthralling voice.

Jenna was the one, the love of his life.

Then, Clark met Ashley. She had hypnotic eyes.

Ashley was the one, the love of his life.

Then, Clark met Tracy. She had mesmerizing breasts.

Tracy was the one, the love of his life.

Then, Clark met Patty…

Planet Submission

"... and that is why you're submissive to me," Clara said.

"That's ridiculous," Mark said, befuddled.

"And yet you're still submissive so..."

"... it must be true."

"Exactly."

"Did you just convince him he's submissive because of a planetary alignment?" Clara's sister whispered in her ear.

"Last week it was because he's a Patriots fan," Clara grinned.

Yes or No?

"Yes or no?" Marjorie asked.

"Yes or no to what?" Saul inquired.

"Yes or no?"

"What is the question?"

"Yes or no?"

"No."

"So you don't want to be my hypnoslave?"

"No, I mean, yes."

"Yes or no?"

"Yes."

"I'm glad you agreed to strip for me now."

"No... I... yes."

He was glad, too.

Breaking a Record

"I can't believe it's been one hundred days since my last orgasm," Cameron remarked.

"Wow, I didn't know you had it in you," His brother, Darren, said.

"It's all Melissa's doing."

"Oh... Chastity device?"

"Hypnosis."

"Yikes! Any other kinks I should know?"

"I'm craving cock right now... Run!"

Darren broke the 100 meters world record.

Uneventful

"How was Mandy's hypno-party last Saturday?" Mark inquired.

"Uneventful," James replied.

"Is that so?"

"Yeah. She used a special microphone to put us under, and an orgy ensued. The police were called in and became a part of it all. I have some pictures. Look."

Mark's jaw dropped.

"Like I said, uneventful," James concluded, yawning.

Hard Limits

"Pass me the salt," Evelyn commanded.

Trevor obeyed.

"Hump the table," Evelyn commanded.

Trevor obeyed.

"Crawl under the table and lick my shoes," Evelyn commanded.

Trevor obeyed.

"Does he do everything you command?" Her mother asked.

"Almost everything. He's my hypnoslave but he has a few hard limits."

"Such as...?"

"He still doesn't eat spinach."

Name of Submission

Friday the 13th. Unlucky to some, but not to him.

He loved it. She had chosen it, after all.

Everything else was irrelevant. Only her words mattered, her control, the trance oblivion in her fingertips.

Glancing at the mirror, he imagined his birth name floating away and moaned, blissfully.

He was Friday, her thirteenth slave.

The Cult

FBI Assistant Director Walter Dales looked at Agent Clark.

"Well?"

"The cult has been dismantled, sir, and everyone freed from the influence holding them captive."

"Then why do the last pages of your report just repeat the sentence I must obey Mistress Cassiopeia?"

"Because it's true," Clark smiled sheepishly, her voice echoing in his thoughts.

English Lessons

"Tell me about Giuseppe..." Mara asked.

"He's wonderful," Bonnie noted. "Didn't know a word of English so I've been teaching him. Giuseppe dear, repeat what I taught you today."

"I am Bonnie's hypnotized boot bitch," Giuseppe droned.

"Nice. Anything else?"

"Oh yes... Giuseppe?"

"I have the chloroform, my Mistress," he said.

Mara's world went black.

Emotional Control

"Jackie?"

"Yes, Bob?"

"I know you're trying to make me angry to control my actions but, this time around, you're only making me sad."

"Sad of losing me?"

"Yes."

"Sad at the thought we may never talk again?"

"Yes."

"If you obey me, you won't be sad because obedience is pleasure and..."

"... happiness."

"Good boy."

Rainbow

"Wake up now," Gloria snapped her fingers.

Neil's eyes fluttered, and he laughed. Where once there was black and white and nothing but extremes, now lived a conflagration of colors, possibilities, and choices, all heightened by the beauty of her eyes.

"You're the rainbow in my cloud," he said.

"You're a rainbow too," she smiled.

Soul in His Mind

"Recognize it?" Laura asked.

"The Soul Stone..." Nathan gasped. "It allows the user to steal, control, manipulate, and alter living and dead souls."

"So if I use it on you...?"

"I'll be your thrall," he drooled.

"Exactly."

Laura deepened the trance, grinning. The imagination of a comic book fan is a terrible thing to waste.

Best Laid Plans

Jackson looked at his brother, tied down to a stone stab.

"I told you I had a plan to leave this wretched ruin, didn't I?

"You forgot to mention it would involve a demon stealing my mind!"

"I also forgot to mention she stole mine too," Jackson shrugged.

They would never forget to obey her.

Mature Relationship

Jack stumbled to the bed, eyes defocused, thoughts fuzzy.

"This is not what I had in mind," he muttered.

"You said you wanted a mature relationship so I'm giving you one… the hypnosis is just to keep you docile. Now, be a good boy and follow my lead," Martha declared.

"Yes, mom," he drifted away.

Relentless

Darren stared at the wall, trapped in vacant eyes. He hated that African tribal mask until Jane had told him to love it.

"When I'm not here, she is your Mistress. Worship her," she commanded.

Darren stared at the wall, trapped in vacant eyes.

The mask wore his mind until it collapsed on the floor.

What in Carnation?

James looked at the red carnation on Cassandra's hair.

"Lovely," he noted.

"It smells nice, too," She urged him.

"Hmmm..."

"What? Afraid I hid a hypnotic in the fragrance? That would be ridiculous, don't you think?"

"I do."

"So do I which is why it was in the glass of wine you had at lunch..."

Crazy Dream

"I had a crazy dream last night," James said.

"Did you?" Tera cooed. "Tell me more."

"I dreamt you were a succubus, looking for a free meal."

"Hmmm... funny, I had a similar dream."

"Really?"

"Yes, I had seconds and went for thirds before you woke up."

"I'm still dreaming, aren't I?"

"Maybe..." she winked.

Colors of the Mind

Blue. The color of her eyes.

Pink. The color of her skirt.

Gold. The color of her pocket watch.

Brown. The color of his eyes.

White. The color of his thoughts.

Black. The color of her strap-on.

Green. The color of his panties.

Red. The color of his lipstick.

Silver. The color of his collar.

Who Says it's the First?

"Mom, I brought the flowers you as… oh God, what are you wearing?" Samuel asked.

"A PVC catsuit, obviously," Gail grinned.

"It's Mother's Day, not Dominatrix Day!"

"Well, I'm a Dominatrix. And a Hypnodomme as well."

"What? How come it's the first time I'm hearing this?"

"Who says it's the first?" She snapped her fingers.

Conclusion

How is your concentration now? Are you totally focused on her needs or do you need a refresher? Read these pieces as many times as you need to get you in the right mood. If you want even more mesmerizing creations, please visit my personal website - https://www.sbspellbound.net - and consider supporting my endeavors so I can keep on going. Thank you in advance.

www.ingramcontent.com/pod-product-compliance
Lightning Source LLC
Chambersburg PA
CBHW031133160726
47989CB00017B/2914